KNIT, PURL, SLIP

A NOVELLA

JAMES JAKINS

Jack Bloodfist
Fixer

Thunder's War
Son of Thunder

Broken Redemption
Knights of the Dead God

Tales From Summervale
First Fixer

For Trev, who only asked for one character that could knit.

INTRODUCTION

We do an annual gift exchange in my family. When the holiday season rolls around we all draw names so we only have to buy a gift for one person instead of everybody.

I'm trying to make it a tradition that every year I write a novella for whichever family member I get.

We draw the names in October, so I'm able to spend my November(NaNoWriMo, for those familiar with the event) working on the book.

This story is the second time I've done this, and is based on the notes my sister gave me. I don't think it's exactly what she had in mind when she asked for a character that knits, but I'm pretty pleased with the end result.

I had a lot of fun writing this little story, and I think that shows. I just hope it's as much fun to read.

CAST ON

THE RAIN FELL hard and fast, filling the gutters along the empty street, washing away the dust and detritus of the slum.

The young woman carried a red umbrella. The water beat against the fabric before rushing down its side in steady streams. She wore a long red coat, a match for her umbrella, and black boots stark against the porcelain skin of her legs. Under the coat she wore a dress of pale blue and modest cut. A scarf, knitted from a red deeper than that of umbrella or coat, was wrapped around a slender neck and hid half a face, leaving only a nose with a history of too many breaks and eyes of a brown closer to red.

If anyone had been on the street with her they would have immediately known she did not belong in this part of the city. This part of the city was for those with no hope.

And it was, occasionally, a place for monsters.

She approached a building, a tenement. Narrow and leaning, with windows broken and a door held in place by one bent hinge.

"Are you there?" a voice asked. The small earpiece is hidden below black hair cut chin length.

"I'm here," she answered.

"Okay, math says they should be on the third floor." The voice is fast. Precise. No syllable wasted.

"Does it now?"

There was the sound of pencil scratching on paper before the answer came. "Yes. With an eighty-five percent certainty."

She let out a short laugh. "I know. I'd never question your math. I'm heading up now."

Another voice cut in. Low and feminine. "Give the word when you're in place."

"Yes, Ma'am."

She took the steps two at a time, silent as the creaking wood allowed.

She heard them before she reached the landing. The snorting and snuffling of wide noses. The scraping and scratching of long claws.

She stopped ten steps short of the landing. Light from the street filtered in through a broken window casting the shadow of one of the figures.

One of the Ravels. Houndlings, from the sound of it.

"In range," she whispered.

The shadow stopped, head turning toward her.

"Ready?" the voice in her ear asked.

"Yes." She lowered her still open umbrella and closed it and held it in front of her in one hand like a sword.

The order came. "Cast on."

The scarf around her neck whipped up, as though tossed by an unfelt breeze and she breathed in that phantom wind. "Casting on."

She leaped the last ten steps and landed in a graceful slide in front of the Ravel.

The creature—a large, fur covered monstrosity—spun its head in surprise.

Before it could let out a warning growl for the rest of its pack she jabbed the point of her umbrella into its chest. The cry that had started as a challenge turned into a pained scream. In and out, twice she stabbed before jumping and flipping over the monster. While in the air the stiletto blade of her umbrella was plunged repeatedly into the fur covered body. Front and back. Knit and purl.

The first Ravel fell to its knees, then stomach, and fell still.

She spun to face the charging pack. Not all houndlings. The first in line was covered in scales, its humanoid form trailed by a thick, lizard tail. A dracon. The math hadn't predicted this.

It opened its mouth and a stream of viscous liquid sprayed toward her.

With a casual flick of her wrist the umbrella popped open, blocking the corrosive acid. Another flick and she sent a glob back toward her attacker and was rewarded with a pained scream as the substance struck the creature in the eyes.

She sidestepped and the still charging, now blind, monster rushed past, stopping only when it hit the nonexistent glass of a window.

A new scream echoed up as it fell to the empty street below.

Umbrella closed, she darted in toward the three remaining beasts. Scarf still trailing behind, swept up by nonexistent winds, she moved as fast as that wind.

In and out her blade moved. Knit, knit, purl, slip. Blood and acid mingled on the ground.

The last Ravel fell to the ground. She stood in her fencing stance for a few minutes, waiting for more, waiting for one of the bodies to shift. There was no movement.

She let out a shaky breath and her scarf fell back to its natural position. She reached up and touched the earpiece, bringing it back to life.

"Bind off," she said.

———

Naald's capital city of Gebreide sits on the small continent's western shore. It is far from the biggest city in the world, but it is the biggest its small nation has to offer.

For miles around the horizon is unbroken rolling hills of green grass. Most of these hills are spotted with the country's greatest export: The sheep.

No other country in the world has native sheep and only Naald's naturally tame landscape is friendly enough for the wool covered animals to thrive.

Several miles from the city was a farm much smaller than many of its neighbors. The Verels were not the wealthiest of shepherds, but they had a loyal, albeit small, client base.

Abigail Verel was waist deep in bleating wool when he showed up. She heard the truck on the other side of the thin wooden wall that protected the sheep from the seaside wind.

She recognized the way the tires crunched the gravel. *It's not weird,* she told herself. *Any girl can recognize the sound of a truck.*

She knew it was a lie and didn't care.

She waded through the mass of sheep and peered around the wall at the gravel path that passed the field she was in and travelled up to the small house that worked double duty as the family home and the business office.

It *was* his truck.

But he wasn't alone. Abigail froze at the side of the wall. She'd been about to rush up the hill to the house. With the winding nature of the road she'd likely make it to the house before the truck so she could be the one to help him, but now she wasn't sure she wanted to. There was a woman in the passenger seat with him.

She did look a little older, though. Maybe his mom? No, not that old. Older sister? Yeah, that had to be it.

She fought her way out of the herd and rushed up the hill. She didn't bother closing the gate. If any sheep did get out they'd make their way back to the pen at watering time, just like they always did.

She made it to the house just seconds before the truck turned the final corner. She rushed around to the back so it wouldn't look like she'd raced the whole way.

She burst in through the back door and her parents looked up in shock.

"Abi?" her father asked, voice concerned. "What's wrong? You look like you saw a ghost."

"He's here," she breathed heavily. She tried to take a deep breath, but it went in shaky and came out loud.

"Oh." Her father sat back down and picked up the morning paper he'd been reading. "Well, you better get to the front desk then. I know how much you love helping around the shop." His tone said exactly what it needed to. That he knew she actually hated working the shop, but she liked *him*.

It wasn't her fault he had a perfect jawline and occasionally wore that thin cotton shirt that didn't completely cover his abs if he raised his arms over his head.

She hoped she'd remembered to put the special order on the top shelf again. She'd been very careful in the few months this particular client had been shopping with them that he had never seen the step-ladder behind the counter.

"Oh, I'm just so short, would you please get it for me?"

Then he'd reach up and—

"Abi?" Her mother's voice broke her concentration. "I heard the bell, you should get up there."

She let out a squeak of alarm and hurried through the house to the front room, which acted as the store-front.

And there he was, waiting patiently at the front counter. His ice-blue eyes lit up when he saw her—She was *not* imagining that.

"Hey, Abigail." His grin. Oh, Shepherd Prince, his grin.

"Hey, Johan." She knew she was grinning like an idiot, but didn't care. She went to lean casually on the counter and almost missed, just catching herself from biting the wooden surface.

Johan either didn't notice or pretended not to.

It took Abigail a moment to register the other person in the room. *Oh, right. His sister.*

The woman was definitely older than Johan. Abigail guessed he was a little over twenty, but wasn't actually sure. He couldn't be more than a few years older than her eighteen.

The woman looked to be in her thirties. She was wearing a fashionable red coat and a knitted scarf of a slightly deeper red. Her straight black hair was cut to just below her jawline. The only feature that some might find unattractive about the woman was her nose. It had been broken before. Possibly multiple times. But it fit the woman so well that Abigail couldn't call it a blemish in any way.

Abigail really hoped she was Johan's sister.

The woman in red was browsing the selection of

wool on display, both the pre-spun, and the large bundles of un-spun. Some dyed, some still the natural color.

She paused beside one of the spinning wheels on display and traced a graceful finger over the wood.

"Oh, Abigail," Johan said, noticing her staring at his companion. "This is my, uh, friend, Melissa."

Abigail's heart sank at the way Johan hesitated before saying "friend."

Melissa looked up from inspecting a rack of spindles. "Melissa Kane. You must be Abigail Veral." Her voice was exactly what Abigail had expected. Light, lilting, and perfectly feminine. She was really starting to hate this Melissa Kane.

Melissa crossed the distance and held a hand out to Abigail.

The younger woman forced a smile and accepted the offered hand. "So nice to meet you. So, what can I help you both with today? I'm guessing you're here for your normal order, Johan?" She looked to Johan, trying to keep her face appropriate for customer service.

"We are," Melissa answered for him. "But I also wanted to speak to you."

"Me?"

"You are the one who spins our order, correct?"

"Our order?" Abigail asked, looking back and forth between the two.

"Forgive me." Melissa smiled, and Abigail did not like the knowing look in the woman's eyes. "I'm Johan's employer. He works for me and my team. Best little gopher we've ever had." She raised a gloved hand and patted Johan affectionately on his perfect cheek.

His face reddened slightly and he tried to move away from the hand.

Melissa turned back to Abigail and bent in close. Her voice was so low that Abigail had to lean in to hear her. "He's single, you know."

Abigail couldn't help herself, she let out a surprised gasp.

Melissa grinned before speaking more loudly. "I came along today because I wasn't sure Johan could place the order correctly."

Johan's blush deepened.

"It's not that I don't trust him, it's just that he doesn't know wool as well as this order would require."

Abigail gawked at that. From the few conversations she'd had with Johan, he knew plenty. The first time he'd come into the shop he'd asked questions that she'd been unable to answer, and she'd been around sheep and wool her entire life. Her father had answered those questions and when Johan had left with a truck bed full of samples, he'd turned to Abigail's mother and said "That boy knows his stuff." Abigail's father did not compliment easily.

"Okay..." Abigail said, slowly.

"Are you familiar with the term *toowerver?*"

Abigail's breath caught in her chest. How did this woman know that word?

"I knew it." Melissa turned to Johan. "Good work, Johan. You were right."

"Told you," he said.

"I don't understand," Abigail said.

"But you do. I could tell right away when Johan brought us those samples. And every one of our custom orders. They've all had just that smallest trace."

Abigail was breathing faster. This was bad. She'd thought she'd been careful. Thought she'd kept it out of her work. But now they were here. Witchhunters. Melissa probably had a pair of the long scissors that marked one of that office.

"I would like to hire you," Melissa said.

Abigail took a gasping breath. "What?" she managed.

"We've been able to make do with our normal orders for a while, but our seamstress is demanding more specialized materials. I was hoping I might convince you to help with that."

"Your seamstress?"

Melissa smiled wider. "It's just a fancy word she likes us to use. Really she's just a knitter." She paused. "Well, I probably shouldn't say *just*. She's actually very good." She lifted one end of her scarf and showed Abigail.

There was something about the scarf that made Abigail look closer. The pattern seemed unusual, but she couldn't place it at first.

Then she saw. "Oh," she said.

There was no way Melissa was a witchhunter. Not while wearing a scarf knitted with magic.

IT HADN'T TAKEN much convincing for Abigail's parents to let her go with Melissa and Johan.

Melissa had spoken to them briefly and told them she wanted to offer their daughter a job within her organization.

Abigail had still been in a sort of shock at discovering that Melissa had been wearing toowerver wool to dispute this when her parents asked her for confirmation.

There had also been the prospect of riding in the truck with Johan. In the *middle* seat, right next to Johan.

Melissa had insisted that she couldn't sit anywhere other than the window seat and that Abigail would have to take the middle. "I'm so sorry about that," she'd said, with a conspiring wink.

Abigail decided that no matter what this so called job offer was, she loved Melissa.

The drive was more awkward silence than Abigail would have liked, but every time the truck hit a bump or dip in the winding road into Gebreide her arm would bounce into Johan's and she did her best to burn the memory of how he felt into her brain.

Melissa spoke, of course. Explaining to Abigail exactly what it was they needed from her.

"We need a lot of yarn, you see. And we need a lot more toowerver wool than we currently have. We thought it might be beneficial to have someone in house to produce it."

"But, why would you need so much?" Abigail asked. "And why me?"

"You, because even the wool you hadn't intended to

imbue with power came away from your wheel with power. Our seamstress was impressed."

"But why do you need it?" Abigail pressed.

Melissa gave her a smile. "It's all perfectly safe. I assure you."

Abigail hadn't thought that it might be something dangerous. Not until Melissa had reassured her. At that point she was convinced there was something very unsafe going on.

No amount of questioning would get either Melissa or Johan to give her an answer, though.

Abigail didn't spend much time in the city, but even she knew what constituted a bad neighborhood.

The street Johan parked on was a half a step above that.

The building was squat and gray, with the only entrance a large rolling garage door.

Its neighbors were a three-storied building with a sign reading "Condemned" across the door and an empty lot filled with broken bottles and yellowing grass.

"Here we are," Melissa said, holding out a hand to help Abigail down from the cab of the truck. "Home sweet home."

"For now," Johan said as he threw a massive bundle of wool out of the truck bed and over his shoulder.

"For now?" Abigail asked. Something about Johan's tone told her he wasn't a fan of the building.

"We move occasionally. We've been in Gebreide for almost half a year and plan on moving on once our work is done here."

"You still haven't told me exactly what that is," Abigail said.

"It's not important, and," Melissa stopped before the door and turned to face Abigail, "I think it's probably better if you're not fully aware of it. We need your help and it's easier if you do your work here, but please, don't ask too many questions."

She tapped the door with the tip of her umbrella.

A few seconds later the door rolled up to reveal one large room made almost entirely of concrete and metal sheets. Several vehicles were parked along the far wall and pallets and crates were scattered around the ground in a haphazard manner.

A young girl that Abigail placed at maybe twelve or thirteen was standing in the doorway with hands on her hips glaring at Melissa. "What took you so long?"

Her voice threw Abigail and forced her to look closer. Despite only reaching Abigail's chest, the girl wasn't actually as young as she'd initially thought. She might even have been the same age as Abi. She was short and slender and all awkward angles. She had skin darkened and eyes a deep green. One eye had a small crescent scar under it that ran from the bridge of the nose and under the wild blond hair that framed her face.

"I told you we were going to be a while," Johan said, walking past and dropping his load of wool on the floor just inside the building.

Melissa indicated to Abigail that they should enter.

"Did you at least remember to stop at that Buiteland

place?" the girl asked Johan, completely ignoring Melissa and Abigail.

"I'll go grab your curry later, okay?" Johan said as he hit the button to lower the door.

She glared at Johan and pulled a fist back to punch the young man.

Melissa caught the upraised hand. "Marcella, this is Abigail. Why don't you say hi?"

The short girl looked over her shoulder as if just seeing the two of them. "Oh, hey, Mel." She gave Abigail a hard look. "This the witch?"

Abigail decided to not take offense at the impoliteness. "Hi, Marcella. It's nice to meet you."

"Marcy. Call me Marcy. Only Mel calls me Marcella." She sneered when she said her full name, as though it tasted awful in her mouth.

She wrenched her arm away from Melissa, though it looked like the older woman had let her, and turned to face Abigail. "Abi, huh? Good to meet you, I guess."

"Marcella, would you be a dear and take Abigail to meet Alma? I'm going to help Johan get this wool into the storeroom."

Marcy glanced over her shoulder at Johan who was lifting the bundle of wool back up and heading toward a small door on the other end of the room.

Abigail recognized the look in Marcy's eyes and felt an immediate rivalry with this girl. She would have to make sure to never leave her alone with Johan.

"Sure, I guess." Marcy shrugged and turned away from Johan, eyes only leaving him when her body was fully facing Abigail. "Come on, Abi." She waved Abigail after her and headed in the opposite direction of Johan.

"So, what's your story?" Marcy asked without looking at Abigail.

"What do you mean?"

"Mel said you're a witch. That true?"

"Not the word we use," Abigail said.

"So you are?" Marcy glanced over her shoulder, her expression almost curious.

"I guess." Abigail shrugged.

"But you can do magic?"

"Toowerver, yeah."

"Toowhatsit?"

"It's just another word for magic, I guess."

"Cool." Marcy seemed to have exhausted her curiosity just as she stopped in front of the door. "Alma's through there."

"I just—"

"Yeah, I'm gonna go help Mel and Jo." Marcy waved at the door and turned to go.

"Okay..." Abigail watched Marcy go for a moment, considering following. In the end she opened the door and stepped inside.

The room was dim and warm. While the previous room had been utilitarian and functional this one felt lived in and comfortable.

The single window had thick curtains drawn leaving the only light in the room to come from, of all things, a fireplace.

A plush armchair was set close to the fire. A large,

brick of a woman sat in the chair. Even sitting down it was obvious she was tall, and almost just as wide. Hair with as much gray as brown was pulled back in a loose bun. She held a pair of slender needles in her hands and she clicked them together, a look of bored concentration on her face.

She glanced up from her work and saw Abigail.

"Are you Alma?" Abigail asked.

The woman peered at her with close-set blue eyes over a pair of narrow half-moon glasses that were perched on her nose. "I am. And you must be the draaier."

Abigail straightened. "I am." A draaier, or spinner, was a witch that could imbue wool with an element, creating toowerver wool. Many draaier could only do one element, but Abigail had a rare gift of being able to use all the elements. She was really proud of that. It was just a shame that her particular magic was considered evil and was outlawed for some reason.

This gift of hers, and her mother's, was the main reason the family farm did so well. Many of their clients had no idea why the wool worked so well, but they kept coming back for more. Then there were the few clients who knew and paid for very specific wool.

"Wonderful. Please, have a seat." Alma nodded to another armchair across from hers.

Abigail sat down and glanced around the room. Dark wallpaper wrapped the room and framed pictures hung from the walls and over the fireplace. Abigail recognized Alma, Melissa, Johan, and Marcella in many of the pictures. They all looked much younger and there were other people in the pictures as well.

Alma noticed her studying the pictures. "That's my family." She smiled fondly at the images that hung on the walls.

"Family?" Abigail asked.

"Well, I don't have any children of my own." Alma shrugged, still moving her knitting needles. "But these kids might as well be."

Her smile disappeared as she looked back to Abigail. Her voice wasn't unfriendly, however. "I assume Melissa told you what we expect from you."

Abigail nodded. "I still don't know why you need it, though. Melissa didn't want to explain anything."

"Do you need an explanation? I hope she at least explained your compensation."

"She did." It *had* been an impressive amount. "I would really like to know what my wool is going to be used for."

"Been used for. I want you to know that I've never worked with better." She nodded down toward the still-clicking needles.

Abigail recognized the wool. It was dyed in a pattern her mother used a lot. "But you need toowerver wool now?" she asked.

Alma nodded. "The little bit of power you unconsciously imbued in your wool was more than enough for me to work with, but now I'd like to see what you can do when you *try*."

Alma tilted her head toward the corner of the room.

Abigail followed the motion to find a spinning wheel of a dark, red wood sitting in the corner.

"I believe Johan should have left a basket next to the wheel." She indicated with another bob of her head that Abigail should check.

Abigail rose and checked. There was indeed a basket of unspun wool behind the wheel.

"Drag it over here and show me what you can do," Alma said, looking back down to her knitting.

KNIT

IT WAS GOOD WOOL. Not from the Verel farm, but high quality.

Abigail set up the wheel and prepared to start the spinning. "Any requests?" she asked Alma.

"Hm," Alma thought as she continued to knit. "Why don't you just give me a decent length of every element you can do."

"Every?" Abigail asked.

Alma looked up. "Can you do multiple?"

Abigail nodded. "I know them all."

"All?" Alma stopped the needles to stare incredulously at the girl. She started knitting again. "Well, let's see then."

Abigail paused, feet over the treadle, grip loose around the wool. "You won't be able to dye it after I'm done."

Alma raised an inquisitive eyebrow but nodded that Abigail continue.

She spun.

The wool was un-dyed. A clean, off-white. It left Abigail's hand white, but once it was wrapped around the bobbin it had color. She started with fire. It was always the easiest to imbue.

The wool around the bobbin glowed for an instant before fading to a bright, fire orange. She continued with the fire long enough that there was a full two layers on the bobbin before slowing her feet on the treadle and focusing.

She began pedaling again and this time she focused her mind on air. The wool wrapping the bobbin was now a pale sky-blue.

From air she changed to water, the color became a deep green. Then earth. The wool took on a dark-brown, almost black, hue. Then spirit, the wool changing from its off-white to a perfect, unblemished white.

She still had wool left so she kept going. Mixing fire with air to get a warm red. Earth and water for a grass green. And a variation of spirit with each of the others that created, not a paler version of each color, but a more intense orange or green or brown.

She'd filled several bobbins by this point and was about to start doing combinations of three at a time when she ran out of wool.

She reached down for the basket to add more, but it was empty.

When she found no wool she blinked and realized she'd lost track of time.

Alma had her knitting resting in her lap with hands

folded over it. She was smiling fondly at Abigail. "That was very impressive."

"Thank you." Abigail bowed her head to try and hide the sudden flush that came to her cheeks with the compliment.

"Might I ask about the colors?" Alma said.

Abigail looked up. "I know. A more experienced draaier would be able to keep the wool uncolored so you'd be able to dye it whatever color you want. I've tried to perfect that, but I've never been able to. My mother handles any of the orders that call for un-dyed toowerver wool."

Alma shook her head. "I don't think experience has anything to do with it." She was holding one of the full bobbins that Abigail had put to the side. She lifted one end of the thread and rolled it between two fingers. "Amazing..." She sighed and put it down. "A shame I won't be able to use it."

Abigail wilted. "It's not good enough?"

"Oh no, girl, it's perfect!" Alma exclaimed. "I'm definitely going to have to request your services. I just meant, well, I am unable to work with thread with multiple elements. Just a single color is all my meager skills allow."

"Did you knit Melissa's scarf?" Abigail asked.

Alma nodded.

"I don't think I'd call your skill meager, either."

Alma smiled as she picked up her knitting again. "I think you've passed the interview Abigail. Welcome aboard."

"Um," Abigail started, "I still don't actually know what it is you do here."

"You know what a Ravel is, right?" Melissa said as she and Abigail sat on a pair of boxes in the warehouse.

"The monsters?" Abigail said.

Melissa nodded. "They're not naturally occurring. They didn't evolve, anyway. And wherever they show up disaster always follows. We travel the world hunting them."

"But, there aren't any monsters—"

Abigail stopped when Melissa smiled. "There won't be when we're done. Don't worry, nothing you do will put you in any danger, but we need your wool. It's what gives us our edge over the monsters."

"So, do you use the wool to make traps, or..." Abigail glanced at the scarf still around Melissa's neck.

Melissa noticed the scrutiny and nodded. "We fight them. Traps, sometimes, but a lot of the time we just do what we have to."

Abigail moved her gaze from the scarf to Melissa's nose. The nose that had obviously been broken multiple times. Other than that one thing, there was nothing about this slender, graceful woman that made Abigail think she could fight monsters.

But there was the scarf. She couldn't interpret the pattern, but if it was toowerver wool, it must endow the woman with some sort of power.

"You don't have to worry about that, though. All you have to do is spin the wool Alma requests. That's it." Melissa said.

"But I have to do it here?" Abigail asked.

"If that's okay? Alma doesn't want that wheel leaving her possession and—"

"I get it," Abigail interrupted. "That wheel is special, I can tell. I think I can do my thing a little easier with that than with my own wheel, honestly."

"You'll take the job then?"

Abigail nodded. "Yeah. I think I will."

Abigail had to give Melissa credit. She'd obviously timed that question for the exact moment that Johan walked out into the warehouse. How could Abigail say no to the prospect of spending more time around *him*?

"Well, if you're okay with it, you'll just set up shop in Alma's sitting room for now." Melissa did a very good job of pretending not to notice that Abigail had stopped looking at her.

The younger woman was busy studying the girl that was with Johan. *Another* girl? How many were there hiding out in this building?

This one came to Johan's shoulders, which meant she'd be about as tall as Abigail. She had long, straight red hair that fell down to her lower back, and Abigail couldn't tell what color her eyes were because they were hidden behind the glare on the glass of the massive glasses she was wearing.

The girl passed Johan and walked straight toward

Melissa and Abigail. She had her hands clasped in front of her and was flexing her fingers nervously.

"Hi, Melissa," the girl said when she was close enough. She glanced at Abigail and quickly looked at the ground, cheeks reddening slightly.

"Hi, Felicia. Have you met Abigail yet?" Melissa turned to face the girl and offered her a warm smile.

"No. Marcella told me about her, though." She spoke quickly, cutting her words off the instant they left her mouth.

Abigail started to rise to greet the girl properly but an almost imperceptible shake of the head from Melissa prompted her to stay in her seat.

"What can I do for you, Felicia?" Melissa asked the girl.

"Outside of town. A nest."

"I'll get my things." Melissa rose from her seat.

"No!" Felicia almost shouted before taking a quick breath and continuing slower. "No. The math says Marcella should handle this one."

"Does it now?" Melissa narrowed her eyes and looked from Felicia to Marcella, who was watching intently from the still open door that Felicia and Johan had walked through earlier.

"It does." Felicia said, apparently oblivious to the suspicion in Melissa's voice.

Melissa straightened her face and smiled down at Felicia, even though the girl was not looking at her. "You're math has never been wrong that I can recall. I'll talk to Johan about getting a transport ready. If you would get ready in the comms room."

Felicia nodded quickly as Melissa walked past toward Johan.

Abigail watched her go for a moment before looking back to Felicia. The girl was standing directly in front of her now, head tilted as she studied Abigail's face. Her eyes were green, Abigail noted, as the other girl studied her.

After a second Felicia seemed to realize what she was doing and stepped back. She mumbled something that might have been an apology. Then, more loudly, "You can come say hi in the comms room if you want."

With that she spun around and walked away. Her steps were as fast as her voice and with her hands still clasped in front of her it made for a fast and stiff retreat.

A few minutes later Abigail was distressed to see Johan and Marcy climb into one of the vehicles parked in the warehouse and drive off.

"Where are they going?" Abigail asked, walking up to Melissa.

"On a hunt. Marcella hasn't done a solo hunt in a while... I'm a little surprised Felicia thought it was a good idea." She stared after the retreating vehicle before pushing a button next to the open door to close it.

She turned to Abigail, trademark smile returned. "Care to join Felicia and I in the Comms room? You can listen in and see how things are going. Make sure Johan is okay."

Abigail's face felt like a furnace. She hated that she

was so easy to read, but she nodded and followed Melissa through a door and down a hallway.

Melissa opened another door and they entered a dark room. Unlike Alma's sitting room, this one had no light source other than a large monitor that took up one wall, it's glow casting the room in a green hue.

A wall of numbers and letters that Abigail had no hope of interpreting scrolled along the screen.

The rest of the room was disgusting. It was the only word Abigail had for it. Paper bags from different restaurants and glass bottles with brightly colored labels declaring "Unlimited Energy" littered the floor.

There was a table in the center of the room, its entire surface almost completely covered in the same bottles and food wrappers. On one end of the table, the end closest to the screen, Felicia was perched.

She sat, cross-legged and propped up by a few stained pillows. She glanced over her shoulder at the two newcomers and nodded in acknowledgement. There was something different about her, Abigail realized. At first she thought it was just the green knit cap she wore— More toowerver wool, Abigail noted—but it was more than that. She seemed more confident, more at ease. *This is her space,* Abigail realized. *Her domain.*

"Felicia," Melissa said, brushing a pile of garbage off a chair and sitting down.

"Hi, Melissa," Felicia said. She spoke with the same, quick voice, but it was louder, more substantial.

"So, what have we sent the young Marcella hunting today?" Melissa asked.

Abigail found a chair with less garbage than the others and cleared it off before seating herself.

"A Magpie."

Felicia's tone was so matter of fact that Abigail was surprised to see Melissa jump to her feet.

"Are you serious?" Melissa shouted. "You sent Marcella out to face a Magpie? Alone?"

"Not alone. She has Johan." Felicia said, eyes never leaving the scrolling wall of numbers and letters.

"Johan is not a fighter," Melissa insisted. "I'm going."

"If you go now," Felicia said, "Marcy will never be able to hunt alone. The math said so."

"Are you sure?" Melissa asked, hand half raised toward the door.

Felicia picked up a pencil and scribbled on a piece of paper sitting next to her on the table. "Yes. Ninety-eight percent."

Melissa let out a long breath. "Fine. But I will be on comms the entire time."

Felicia nodded. "Don't worry. It'll be fine."

IT HADN'T TAKEN much effort for Marcy to convince Felicia that she could handle this hunt alone.

Marcy knew she could do it. She just had to prove herself. Even if it was apparently a Magpie. But maybe it wasn't. The math wasn't always right.

But even if it was a Magpie, Felicia had done the math. Marcy would be okay. The math was never wrong.

Besides, Johan was with her. She couldn't fail as long as he was there to watch.

She glanced away from the scenery outside her window toward the boy in the seat next to her.

He was a few years older than her sixteen, and he had been in her life almost as long as she could remember. They had been found by Alma at the same time. Melissa had been first, then Felicia, then the two of them. They'd all grown up together.

They all loved each other like siblings.

Marcy didn't like how that new girl, Abigail, looked at Johan. So she'd convinced Felicia to tell Melissa to stay behind, so Johan had to drive. So she could get him away from Abi's hungry eyes.

"You sure you're up for this?" Johan asked, eyes focused on the road. He was driving much faster than the suggested limits on the signs they blurred past. But he was wearing the socks Alma had made him. His reflexes would be improved and Marcy knew he wouldn't drive them off the road, regardless of how rough and un-road-like it had become.

Marcy nodded and grinned. "Come on. You know I got this."

Johan let out a short laugh. "I guess I do."

The drive took longer than Marcy normally would have liked, but it was enjoyable enough with Johan there.

He parked the truck in the shadow of a massive standing rock. "I think this is the place." He checked the map laid out on the dashboard. "The Krans Rocks."

Marcy put her earpiece in and tapped it once. "Hey, Fey, can you hear me?"

"We can hear you," Melissa's voice replied. She did not sound happy. Johan and Marcy exchanged grimaces.

"Hey, Mel. Can you guys check the numbers? We at the right place?"

"Yes," Felicia said. "You're going to have to do some climbing."

"This place doesn't look very well traveled," Johan said after they had both climbed out of the vehicle. "Probably a good thing, knowing how you like to do things."

"Rude," Marcy said.

They both looked up and studied the landscape. The cliff face they had parked beside was one of countless sheer rock-faces. They dotted the landscape like free-standing pillars. Some were topped with large boulders, somehow balanced at strange angles.

"Well," Johan said, "you heard the lady, get climbing. I'll keep the engine running for you."

She rolled her eyes before pulling out the small green bag that she'd kept on the floor for the drive. She opened the top and shifted the never-used knitting needles that Alma always insisted she practice with and the roll of wool that was never going to be knitted into anything. After a little digging she finally found what she was looking for. She hated that Alma always insisted on packing these first. Marcy knew it was an intentional tactic to remind her that she needed to practice her knitting.

She raised the brown knit gloves up and studied them. No catches or tears in the wool. That was good.

She pulled the gloves on her hands and clenched her fists. She was always a little jealous of Melissa and her scarf. How obvious it was that the magic was working. That pretentious wind that always announced the woman was about to kick ass.

But that was okay. She didn't need it.

"See you in a bit." She grinned widely at Johan before jumping onto the hood of the truck.

"Hey! Don't dent it!" Johan shouted after her as she leaped from the truck and into the sheer face of the standing stone.

"Oh, it'll be fine!" She yelled back as she punched a fist through the rock.

She climbed the cliff like that, fist over fist. In a matter of seconds she crested the top of the stone.

With a grunt she pulled herself up the last ten feet and launched up the face and landed with a graceful slide.

She could see it. Across the field of stone columns and oddly angled boulders they saw each other.

Against the gray sky of a storm that wanted to break, the black wings spread and the Magpie sang.

"CASTING ON!" Marcy shouted before anyone on the other end could give the order.

She ran to the edge of the tiny plateau and jumped.

With the strength granted her by her toowerver gloves she cleared the distance between one pillar and the next with almost no effort.

The instant she landed on the next she placed her next foot down and pushed back into the air.

Skip, jump, land, skip, jump, land. In this way she cleared the distance between her and the Magpie.

The monster did not wait idly, however. As soon as it had finished its eerie song it had flapped its wings and dove toward the girl that was skipping toward it.

They met in the middle of the field of standing stones and boulders.

Marcy jumped one final time, straight up, as the feathered monster angled its flight down.

The Magpie looked like a man. Covered in black feathers with hands that held talons rather than fingers. From the broad back sprouted two wings, the span enough to blot out the sun if the clouds were not already doing so.

The head a smooth, white bone with a long, hooked beak aimed for Marcy's throat.

Marcy smashed her right fist into the monster's temple and sent it through the air to her left.

Her gloves could punch through stone, but they did nothing to the thick bone that protected the Magpie's head.

The Magpie spun wildly for a moment before wings snapped out, cracking the air, and it regained itself.

It tucked the wings behind its back and it dove below Marcy's field of vision, into the forest of stone pillars.

Marcy rushed to the edge of her cliff and glanced down.

While she searched for the monster it tackled her from behind and carried her away from the safety of solid ground.

She cursed and twisted in place as talons ripped her clothing.

She managed to get enough momentum that she spun around, the fabric of her shirt tearing entirely free of the Magpie's grip.

Still spinning, she threw another punch, this time connecting with the arm reaching to grab her.

There was the sound of breaking bone and the Magpie threw its head back, smaller beak under the bone-white one, open in a scream.

The cry of pain echoed off the stone walls as Marcy fell among them.

Her fall was not perfectly straight, and she was relieved that her trajectory took her near enough to one of the sheer rock faces.

She grabbed at the wall and her fingers dug into the stone. She fell a few feet, leaving five long grooves in the rock before stopping completely.

The sound of an angry cry was her only warning and she had just enough time to get her feet up underneath her and push away from the rock.

The surface of the pillar dissolved as the Magpie's beak struck the stone.

Marcy hit the nearest cliff and latched on, grip digging into stone, and she quickly began to climb. She moved like a frog. Throwing herself up and grabbing with both hands at once, then pulling up and repeating the motion. Each vertical leap carried her ten feet or more.

She was almost to the top when another angry cry announced the approach of the Magpie. Instead of continuing her upward climb she jumped off the rock face and launched backward.

She flew underneath the form of the winged monster. It attempted to spin, mid-flight, to intercept her, but it just spun in the air and crashed into the pillar Marcy had just left.

She landed with no grace on a lower pillar. She took a moment to catch her breath, eyes never leaving the form of the Magpie as it shook itself from the shock of its crash.

She didn't get much time to recover before the Magpie launched off the stone and dove toward her.

"Seriously?" she turned and jumped.

She landed on the top of the egg shaped boulder just as the Magpie's talons scored along her back.

She cursed as she rolled forward, managing to dodge most of the blow.

She touched a gloved hand to her back and it came away wet. The brown wool of the gloves sodden with blood and the grit of broken stone.

The Magpie was circling above, preparing for another dive.

Marcy was really regretting not bringing Mel along for this one. The woman always seemed to have a plan. She probably would have figured out some way to trap the Magpie before dropping a boulder on top of it.

Marcy blinked. That wasn't half bad.

The Magpie let out another cry as it aimed its beak toward Marcy and plummeted toward her.

She jumped again. She didn't stop this time. Just moved from pillar to pillar. Every time she landed with more force, less control.

She hoped that to the monster it looked like she was running away. She moved as fast as she could to keep up that illusion.

It no longer rose above her in an attempt to dive, but instead stayed even with her, taloned hands reaching toward her. Before long it was flying below her, weaving in and out of the pillars, waiting for her to slow down.

With the gift of her gloves she was able to push herself just enough that she was able to gain a lead against the Magpie.

She landed roughly on a pillar and was rewarded with the sound of cracking stone. The boulder balanced on top of it had been knocked loose from its perfect setting.

She leaped quickly off the boulder into the nearest pillar and launched herself back toward the now tipping boulder.

She landed on top of it and pushed it back in the opposite direction.

There was another loud crack as the base of the pillar crumbled and the entire structure began to fall.

She let out a joyous cry at the sight of the Magpie attempting to change direction mid-flight.

The boulder struck the monster square in the back and it, and the pillar, carried the Magpie to the ground.

Marcy rode the rock all the way down, fists raised over her head as she screamed for the whole world to hear.

"BIND OFF!"

PURL

"Did something happen?" Abigail asked.

Melissa shook her head. "We have no way of knowing. The Magpie sang. No radio signals are going to get through the area until Marcella does her job." She almost looked flustered as she leaned back in her chair and folded her arms.

From one corner of the room shape shifted and Abigail jumped in surprise.

A dog rose with a wide yawn and padded over to Melissa and placed its head in her lap.

"Hi, Beans," she said, petting the animal's golden head without looking at it.

"What is that?" Abigail asked.

Melissa looked at her like she was crazy. "It's a dog, Abigail."

"I know, sorry, I just meant, what breed is he?"

"Oh." Melissa looked down at the animal with a look

of confusion that seemed unnatural for her. "I don't actually know. Felicia?"

"Hm?" Felicia looked over her shoulder at Melissa, Abigail and Beans. At the sound of her voice Beans lifted his head from Melissa's lap and made his way over to Felicia.

"What breed is Beans?" Melissa asked.

"Oh. Beansie is something called a Lab." Her voice was much more animated than Abigail had heard so far. The girl bent down and took a side of the dog's head in each hand and moved them up and down in a way that made his tail thump against the floor.

"I've never heard of that," Abigail said.

"That's because my Bean is the only one ever, huh, Beansie?"

With a long red tongue hanging from one side of his mouth he let out a short bark.

Abigail gave Melissa a confused look, hoping she would be able to explain a little more than the obviously distracted Felicia.

"Felicia and Beans came to us on the same day," Melissa explained. "I don't know where she got him."

"Jack gave him to me," Felicia answered. Her voice had returned to its normal fast-paced calm. Her hands hadn't left the dog's face, however, and the animal was beaming up at her.

"That's right. How could I forget?"

"Who?" Abigail asked.

Melissa shrugged. "I never met him, but he, well, he saved Felicia from a monster when she was very young."

"A Ravel?" Abigail asked.

"No," Felicia answered. "He saved me from the Selvage."

"The... Selvage?"

Melissa gave Felicia a look that Abigail was sure the girl could feel through the back of her skull. She was apparently less than pleased with this revelation.

"Yes." Felicia was scribbling furiously on her piece of scrap paper. "I was only five. The Selvage came to my house. He brought all his monsters. His Houndlings and Dracons and Magpies. They killed everybody. But Jack got there just in time to save me."

"Selvage... are real?" Abigial was only half listening to Felicia's story. She was too caught up in the fact that Felicia had just told her that the biggest, most feared monsters were not only real, but could just show up and kill an entire family.

Felicia nodded, not letting the interruption distract from her story. "After Jack killed the Ravel and chased the Selvage away he told me he had a new family for me. One that would help me get revenge. I was only five and that scared me."

"And he gave you the dog?" Abigail asked.

"He asked if I'd be less scared if I had someone to always protect me. I said yes. He left me alone for a little bit and came back with Beans. Beans was just a puppy. Small, like me. But Jack said he was a smart dog and that he would always stay by me and protect me. Said he was the only dog like him in the whole world. That he was special. Like me." Felicia seemed to zone out for a moment, just petting Beans, who didn't seem to mind at all. "Then he took me to Alma and Melissa."

Melissa's smile was sad when she spoke. "It was just Alma and I back then. I was so excited to have a little sister. So happy that I wouldn't have to be alone when fighting the monsters."

Abigail wasn't sure if it would be appropriate to ask for more information, so she remained silent. Melissa seemed to sense the unspoken question, though.

"The Selvage killed my family, as well. Alma's too. And Marcella's, and Johan's. Alma had been chasing him ever since he killed her family. She found me just a day too late. We tracked him for years before Felicia joined us. Marcella and Johan came a few years later. The Selvage burned down their orphanage."

"And now he's here," Felicia finished.

"Why?" Abigail asked.

Melissa shook her head. "I don't know what you know about the Selvage. They're the first monsters. Some legends state that they're the first sentient beings to live on this world. All we really know is that they feed off the pain and anger of humans. They look human, so it's almost impossible to find them, at least until they start their killing."

Abigail considered that. "They feed off pain? How?"

"I don't know. But this one? He's hungry. I'm sure you hear the news reports. Even outside the city on your farm."

Abigail nodded. It seemed like there was always something going on. Nowhere in the news reports was it ever mentioned that Ravel were involved, but she found that she believed Melissa that there were monsters in the city.

"I'd understand if you wanted to get out of the job," Melissa said.

Abigail looked up in surprise. "Why would I do that?"

"You're not scared?"

Abigail shook her head. "Terrified. But if I can help I'd kind of be a horrible person if I refused, don't you think?"

Before Melissa could answer a voice crackled over the suddenly active radio. "BIND OFF!"

The relief that suddenly filled Melissa's face confirmed for Abigail that she needed to help these people.

WHEN MARCELLA and Johan returned from their hunt Melissa pulled Felicia and Marcella into a room.

Abigail couldn't make out the specific words, but the tone was very obviously angry.

Turned out that Felicia had lied about the other girl's chances of survival. At Marcy's request she'd convinced Melissa to let her go alone.

"I warned her it was a bad idea," Johan said.

He and Abigail were sitting at the table in Felicia's conference room with the old dog, Beans, on the floor between them, breathing heavily as Abigail scratched his head.

"Why'd she risk that?" Abigail asked.

"She had to prove herself, I think. She's always been the backup, you know? Had to show everyone she could do it."

"So, is Melissa in charge?"

Johan laughed at that. "Shepherd, no. I mean, sort of. Alma's in charge and since Mel's the oldest she's sort of the de-facto second-in-command, but there really isn't a command structure or anything. We all just sort of do what we're good at."

"And you?"

Johan's smile wavered. "I've never been very good at fighting, but I like to drive so I do the shopping and any other chores the others don't want to deal with themselves."

The door opened and Alma entered the room.

She approached Abigail and Johan and slowed when she heard muffled anger through the wall. "What's going on in there?"

"Marcy convinced Felicia to send her on a hunt alone," Johan answered.

"How'd she do?" Alma asked.

"Destroyed half of the Krans Rocks, but she killed a Magpie."

Alma's eyes opened wide. "A Magpie? Alone?" She smiled. "I knew she had it in her."

A door opened and the three women exited. Felicia and Marcella looked suitably penitent and Melissa was her normal composed self.

Alma strode toward them. She set a hand on Marcella's shoulder and bent down to whisper in her ear.

Marcy's cheeks turned red but she smiled at whatever was said.

Alma straightened and addressed Melissa. "Can I have a word, dear?"

"Of course." Melissa bowed her head and turned to let Alma lead the way into the now vacated room.

"About time she got a lecture of her own," Marcy said, probably a little louder than was really necessary.

Felicia just shrugged before climbing back up to her perch on the edge of the table. She picked up the knit cap that she'd left there and put it on, pulling it down almost past her eyes, as though trying to hide inside it.

"Hey, it's okay, Fey," Johan circled the table and sat next to her. "You know Mel isn't going to hold it against you for long."

Felicia shook her head. "I was dumb. The math was bad. It was only Thirty-two percent. But I lied."

"Don't look at it that way, Felicia," Abigail said.

The others all looked to her. Marcy seemed a little upset that she was butting in where she didn't belong, but Felicia seemed eager to hear what she had to say. Her almost emotionless face still carried a silent pleading for reassurance.

"You just chose to trust Marcy more than your math. I don't see what's wrong with that."

"The math's never wrong," Felicia said.

"Well, it looks like it was this time. And I think you

knew that or you never would have agreed to let her go alone."

Felicia tilted her head and studied Abigail.

Abigail's cheeks heated at the scrutiny.

"You're smart, Abi," she said before apparently pushing the issue from her mind and turning to study her constantly scrolling wall of numbers.

"Was the math really that bad?" Marcy asked. Her face had gone pale.

Felicia nodded.

"But you let me go anyway?"

Felicia flicked her eyes at Marcy before looking away again. "You told me to trust you. I think Abigail's right. I knew you'd be okay."

Marcy jumped on the table behind Felicia and, dropping to her knees, pulled the girl into a tight hug. "Thanks for believing in me, Feyfey."

Felicia sat up straight pulling herself out of Marcy's hug. "Quiet. I need to focus."

She was staring at the screen, eyes open wide behind her thick glasses, her hand moved across her scrap paper apparently independent of her.

"What is it?" Johan asked.

"Sh," she didn't even spare the energy of words to silence him.

From the floor Beans whined nervously. He seemed to be staring at the screen as well.

"Alma! Melissa!" Felicia spun from the screen to the door the two women had entered.

The door slammed open and Alma rushed into the room. "What is it?"

Melissa followed behind. She was her normal composed self except for the red-rimmed eyes.

"A nest. Big. Very big."

"Should I trust you to decide who goes?" Alma asked.

"Everyone. All three of you have to go." Felicia's voice didn't have its normal monotone. It was filled with fear.

Alma cut short whatever she'd been about to say. She just closed her mouth and nodded. "Melissa, Marcella, get your things. Sorry, Marcy, no time to rest."

"Oh, I am ready to go!" Marcy slid off the table and ran out of the room.

"You have coms?" Alma asked.

"Won't work where you're going. It's in the sewers. I drew you a map." Felicia held up the paper she'd been using. Sure enough, a rough map was sketched on it.

"Are we sure this is a good idea?" Johan asked as Felicia and Abigail piled into the truck next to him. Beans was already sitting happily in the back.

"I have to make sure before I tell Alma," Felicia insisted. She was still wearing her cap.

"Didn't the math confirm it, though?" Johan said.

Felicia shook her head. "I don't think all the numbers are accurate anymore. Need to update the system. So we have to confirm this way first."

"Okay." Johan started the truck and drove away from the warehouse.

Felicia had waited until the coms had gone down after the three hunters, Alma, Melissa, and Marcella, had entered the city's sewer system. She'd then informed Johan and Abigail that they had to go into the city.

She claimed the math had found the Selvage.

"I just want it on the record," Johan continued as he guided their vehicle onto a busy thoroughfare, "that I think this is a horrible idea."

"Noted," Felicia said.

"So, just how dangerous are Selvage?" Abigail asked. "I know Ravel are bad, but I haven't really heard *that* much about Selvage."

"They're bad," Johan answered. "Really bad. Alma has been hunting this one almost her entire life. I don't know how dangerous they are physically, compared to Mel and Marcy I mean, but they're smart. I've never actually seen one that I know of. They look human."

"I've seen him," Felicia cut in. "I'll know if it's him."

"That was ten years ago, Fey," Johan said, but the argument sounded weak.

The three of them sat in silence after that. Felicia had already told Johan the name of the place they were going and he knew the city well enough that he took them right there.

"Chelsea Industries?" Abigail asked, looking out the window at the square building that seemed to be made entirely of glass and chrome.

"Yes," Felicia said simply.

Abigail studied the building. Chelsea Industries was the biggest company in Gebreide and likely the entire country of Naald. It had been around for at least as long as she could remember. "What do you think it's doing here?" she asked.

"He owns it." Felicia said, leaning forward in her seat and staring at the front doors of the large building.

"How do you know that?" Johan asked.

"Math."

"That's really convenient," Abigail said.

"Look." Felicia pointed out the window and they followed her instructions.

A tall man with pale skin and slicked back black hair wearing a slim-fitting black suit and tie and a red shirt was standing next to the road.

He was surrounded by men and women, all wearing the same white buttoned shirts and blue suits.

"Is that—" Abigail started.

"It's him." Felicia interrupted. Her voice almost cracked and she had started shaking. She'd pulled her legs up against her chest and was trying to make herself as small as possible.

"I recognize him," Johan said.

Abigail and Felicia looked at him.

He shrugged. "I saw his picture in a newspaper a while ago. That's Ald Chelsea. The owner and founder of Chelsea Industries."

Ald seemed to be having a friendly enough conversation with a young woman carrying a clipboard. The two climbed inside the car parked near them and a few of the suited individuals followed behind them. Then the car drove away.

"Should we follow him?" Johan asked.

Felicia shook her head violently. "No. Let's go back."

ALD CHELSEA SETTLED into the plush seating of his personal transport. His protection detail took their own seats around him. He didn't need the protection, but he liked having more people around. Occasionally he needed a quick snack.

He glanced out the window as the car pulled away. The truck wasn't following, but the three youths inside were definitely watching him go.

He made a mental note of the truck's make and registration numbers, as well as the faces of the two young women and young man inside.

Hunters, he suspected. They seemed very young, but those were the types that usually ended up coming after him. Boys and girls seeking revenge.

He'd never been tracked back to Gebreide before. He thought he'd always covered his tracks well enough to avoid that. It probably had something to do with the increased Ravel activity in the city. He had been allowing the creatures to propagate more than usual. That was fine, though. If he had been discovered he really only had two options. Either he eliminated the group that had found him or he followed through with his contingency plan. It had been almost a millennia since he'd allowed himself an entire city for a feast.

He pushed that from his mind. For now he had to focus on the smaller meal ahead of him.

The driver stopped the car at the address his assistant had provided. He and the woman—He could never remember their names—climbed out of the vehicle and strode down the walkway to the entry of the three-story apartment building.

Crowded around the entrance were all the residents of the building. They were speaking and shouting with each other but fell silent at their approach.

"Are you the sheep-turd that put this up?" one of the tenants shouted, holding up the eviction notice.

He could already taste the anger. It thrilled him.

"Good evening everyone," he said, taking up position in front of the crowd. His voice carried just the right amount of authority to silence the complaining of the crowd.

Around the crowd his security detail, both those that had been in his car and those that had followed behind, were taking up positions around the area.

"My name is Ald Chelsea. I'm sure you've heard of me." More spikes of anger flared around him and he sucked them in, relishing the sharp flavor. Of course they'd heard of him. He owned over half the city. They suspected what was coming next. He knew that. Could feel the start of fear growing. That sweet, mellow flavor started to mingle with the anger.

"I'm so sorry to inform you that this is not a mistake.

Those eviction notices are effective immediately. You have until tomorrow night to clear the premises. Thank you so much for your time."

Emotions. All of them. He took them in and relished every unique flavor and scent. Anger, fear, outrage, confusion, frustration, isolation. They all mingled together into the perfect blend.

Someone in the crowd threw a rock. He could have easily dodged it, but he turned his face, as though to address his assistant and let it hit him in the cheek.

He reeled back, slapping a hand to his cheek, using a fingernail to pierce the skin to sell the act.

More of the crowd cheered and began looking for their own ammunition, but Ald employed the most ruthless security force in the city.

From suit pockets extendable batons were pulled and the men and women in their pristine suits waded into the crowd.

Pain mingled with the other emotions and Ald had to force himself to not close his eyes at the exquisite taste of it.

THE GROUP HAD LOST contact with HQ the instant they'd stepped inside the wet brick of the city's sewers and had relied solely on the crude map Felicia had drawn for them. But as was almost always the case with Felicia's math, the map had led them right to the nest.

The girl had been right that all three of them needed

to be here. Might have undersold the situation, truth be told.

The three of them were crouched inside an opening in the brick tunnel. Before them was a long metal walkway that ran through the middle of a large, round chamber. Below the metal bridge was a deep pit, the bottom of which all but writhed with the forms of Ravel. Dracon and Houndlings.

The ceiling of the chamber extended as far up as it descended down. Three Magpies slept in crevices in the walls.

The three of them consulted silently, Alma gesturing and nodding at each of the young women and toward the monsters.

Each of them signaled their understanding of her instructions.

Melissa adjusted her scarf and the ends were lifted by an unfelt breeze that had no right to be in this stagnant place. She tightened her grip on her umbrella with its needle point tip and nodded.

Marcella flexed her hands, dried monster blood flaking away from the soft wool. She stretched her neck until there was a pop and gave her own nod.

Alma took a deep breath, a blade sharp knitting needle held in each hand. Around her shoulders the gray shawl she wore began to emit a gentle glow. "Cast on," she whispered.

"Casting on," Melissa and Marcella mimicked.

And they moved.

Alma and Marcy rushed down the walkway a short

distance before each leaped over the low handrails, Alma going left and Marcy right.

Both let out a war-cry that echoed in the confines of the circular room.

Above them the Magpies shook themselves awake and flew out of their cracked brick beds.

Melissa darted just past the opening and leaped straight up. The power of her scarf carried her ten feet, almost half the distance to the ceiling. With a graceful flip she kicked herself off the wall and launched herself toward the nearest Magpie as it studied the falling figures of Marcy and Alma.

Whenever she used her scarf time slowed for Melissa. Everything happened in a moment.

Knit!

She drove the needle point of her umbrella through the narrow eyehole in the Magpie's bone-white helmet.

With the blade sticking out of the creature's skull she used her momentum and flipped forward, planting her feet on the feathered back between the massive wings. She wrenched the umbrella free and jumped off the Magpie.

Purl!

The second Magpie didn't have time to register the attack before Melissa's umbrella pierced the base of its skull, where the bone helmet met flesh.

It let out a short cry of surprise before Melissa twisted and sliced the blade through the neck, silencing the monster forever.

She grabbed the falling body and pushed it below her

and used it as a launch pad to send her closer to the final Magpie.

It had turned and was diving toward her, jagged bone beak ready to crush and tear.

Slip!

She twisted in her flight. The Magpie flew past her. Her coat tore as the creature's beak caught the fabric.

She dropped the umbrella from her right hand and caught it in her left, driving the point up into the monster's chest.

The force of the stab spun the monster over so its back was aimed to the ground.

Using the lodged umbrella she pulled herself on top of the falling Magpie.

She pulled the umbrella free and with a flurry of stabs ended the third and final monster.

Time resumed its steady march.

Marcella and Alma hit the ground at the same time.

Marcy landed, fist first and the Dracon that had been watching her descent died instantly.

The girl laid out about her with wild blows. The Ravel were bunched up closely enough that she didn't have to move from her place. She just planted her feet and threw her punches.

When the Houndlings and Dracons directly around her moved away she worked her way in a slowly growing circle, never having to go very far to find a target.

It was easy when they came to her.

Knit!

She punched forward in a straight jab, crushing the snapping jaws of a slavering Houndling.

Purl!

She aimed a sharp elbow behind her and a Dracon fell with a destroyed windpipe, acidic bile foaming from its mouth.

Slip!

A Houndling and Dracon both swiped clawed hands and she slid between the two. With a grunt she snatched the Dracon's tail and smashed the scaled monster into the furred.

Knit, knit, purl, knit, purl, slip, purl, purl, knit. Marcy moved among the monsters. Her small frame quick and powerful. She roared, all her anger, frustration, everything! She put it all in her fists and wrought death and chaos.

At the same instant Marcella had hit the ground, Alma had landed as well. The large woman, nothing but a square brick of muscle, drove her two needles through the skull and neck of two Houndlings.

Behind her a Dracon brought a clawed hand down on her back. It flew away with a pained cry as her shawl burst with a bright gray light.

She quickly pulled her needles out of the Houndlings before ramming a shoulder into another. There was another burst of gray light and the monster flew, lifeless and limp, into another of the Ravel.

She moved herself into the mass of monsters. Needles, held in a reverse grip, finding vital points. Blood misted in front of her as she stabbed and tore with the slender lengths of metal.

Knit, Knit!

She stabbed with one, then the second needle. One in each side of a Dracon's neck an instant before it could launch a spray of acid in her face.

She tore the needles free and swiped the monster away with a vicious backhand.

Purl!

With a speed belied by her size she spun behind a rearing Houndling and drove a needle through its back. The point severed spine and the monster fell limp.

With an almost casual kick she sent it flying into a charging group.

Slip!

She ducked under a swipe from a Houndling. As she moved she dropped the needle in her right hand and snatched it up again. Holding the needle in a natural grip she drove it forward into the Houndling's heart.

She moved like that, fast and strong and unshakable and knit a pattern of death.

Above Alma and Marcy, Melissa and a dead Magpie landed loudly on the metal walkway, the Magpies bone mask ringing the metal like a bell.

Melissa wasted no time in dropping from the bridge. She landed amid the Houndlings and Dracon and her Umbrella darted in and out and around.

The three of them did their work.

Knit, Purl, Slip.

After a time the work was done. They all stood, too

breathless and tired to make any comment at the piles of broken bodies and rivers of blood.

"Bind off," Alma said, finally.

"Bind off," the other two repeated.

ALMA and the others didn't really acknowledge the news that Felicia had found the Selvage. Alma had nodded and mumbled something that might have been "We'll talk later," but the three of them had essentially just gone straight to their individual rooms and collapsed.

Abigail, Felicia, and Johan sat in relative silence in the Math Room, as Abigail had started calling it in her head. It had been several hours since the others had returned and the three of them were growing restless.

Johan was leaning back in a chair, its back against the wall, petting Beans, who would whine anytime Johan removed his hand.

Abigail was rolling the lengths of wool she'd spun for Alma as part of her test into several skeins. Alma had said she wouldn't be able to use the wool, so Abigail had decided to keep it. As a draaier she should be able to use it for something.

Felicia sat in her normal spot, perched on the end of the table. She held her hat in her hands and was practically wringing it.

"Felicia?" Abigail said, tentative.

"Hm?" Felicia didn't look up.

"Can I ask how the math works?"

Felicia waved a hand. "The system pulls data from whatever city we're in. News reports, police records. Jumbles it all together as numbers. When I wear my hat," she held the hat up, "I'm smart enough to interpret the numbers. I can triangulate when and where something's going to happen."

"Oh." She still didn't understand, but at least her theory about what the hat did was confirmed. "Are you going to be okay?" she asked.

Felicia shrugged.

"We're all going to be okay."

The three of them turned, Johan loudly dropped his chair back to all four legs, startling Beans.

Alma stood in the doorway. She looked tired, but alert. "I need you to tell me everything you saw at Chelsea Industries."

It hadn't been much, but they told her everything. Felicia insisted it had been the same man she'd seen as a child. Alma believed her. Felicia had a perfect memory and Alma knew better than to doubt that.

"We'll need to get ready. Melissa and Marcella need rest. They're worn out. Abigail, it's going to be up to you and I to get ready for this. Johan will take you home for the night, but first thing tomorrow morning I want you back here so we can get started. I would not be upset if you spent the night spinning."

"Need anything specific?" Abigail asked.

"Earth, for now. Perhaps some Air, if you have the time. But make sure you rest. The next few days are going to be very rough."

She turned to Johan and handed him a slip of paper. "After you drop Abigail at home I need you to pick up these supplies."

He rose and took the paper. "Yes, Ma'am."

The whole drive back to the farm felt incredibly tense for Abigail. She wanted to ask Johan what was going to happen but she was afraid of the question.

The state that Alma and the others had been in when they'd dragged themselves back into the warehouse had been terrifying. They had been dead on their feet. Covered in blood and grime, and their eyes hand seemed unable to focus.

And now they were going to be going up against something that all legends claimed was the worst monster to ever exist.

Finally she did speak. "What do you know about the Selvage?"

"What do you mean? This specific one or just in general?"

"Both, I guess."

"Well, this Selvage killed Alma's family years ago. She's been hunting him ever since. She adopted all of us after he killed our families, or destroyed our homes. I don't know much beyond that. Well, I guess now we know that he's Ald Chelsea."

"And what about just Selvage? The monsters?"

"Depending on which legends you want to listen to they're either the first, or the last. Some claim both. There are religions from before the Shepherd Prince that even worshipped them as gods. Not really gods, actually. More like ancestors or predecessors. They believed that humans came from them. That we were the weaker children of the Selvage."

"So, they're powerful?"

"Very. From everything Alma's taught me, they're strong, fast, practically indestructible. The thing that really makes them dangerous, though, is that they feed off negative emotions."

"What?"

"Yeah, I know, sounds weird. But stuff like anger, fear, panic. It just makes them stronger. I was doing a little research earlier, and Chelsea is very unpopular in the city right now because he's evicting tenants from buildings he owns. He goes in person to deliver the news. Probably loves that everyone hates him so much if he gets to eat those feelings."

"So, do you think Alma and the others can beat him?"

He forced a smile. "Of course. They have to."

"But they hate him. He killed their families. Won't them facing him just make him stronger?"

His smile vanished and he reached across the distance between them to grasp her hand. "That's why you're here. With your help Alma's going to be able to make everything they need to win."

She squeezed back. "I'll do my best."

"I know. Thank you."

He walked her to the door once they arrived at the farm and they talked for a bit. He tried to change the subject away from Ald Chelsea and what was coming, and she silently thanked him for that.

After he left she wondered if maybe she should have kissed him. Would that have been weird? Probably.

She said good night to her parents and did her best to give vague, uninteresting answers to their questions about the strange job she'd accepted.

Then she climbed the stairs to her room, a bag of the best wool she could find cradled in her arms. She had a wheel set up in her room. It was a special wheel gifted to her by her grandmother, the first draaier in her family. It would serve her well that night.

It was time to spin.

SLIP

IT HAD BEEN THREE DAYS. Three days of almost no sleep and constant work.

Alma had spent that time knitting for herself, Melissa, and Marcella.

Using Abigail's higher quality toowerver wool she had replaced Melissa's scarf. This one still a warm red. The original scarf had been knit using wool imbued with Air, but this was Air and Fire. It would not only increase the girl's speed, but endurance and strength.

Marcella had new gloves. Earth and Water to replace the singular Earth. If Alma's pattern held true it would increase strength and reflexes.

She'd knit for all three of them a shawl. The wool a perfect black. Abigail had managed several skeins imbued with every element. The shawls should provide all of them with a near perfect defense.

She hadn't believed Abigail at first when she'd insisted that the mixtures would work for her knitting, but they had. The girl was skilled. She'd managed to take multiple elements and trick the wool into thinking they were one, which meant Alma could use it with her patterns.

They stood now in front of the tall tower that was Chelsea Industries.

There was a slight drizzle, and all three of them stood together under Melissa's umbrella. Alma's shoulders were too wide for her to remain completely dry, but at least her hair, in it's neat bun, was untouched.

The three of them approached the building.

Melissa holding her umbrella, perfectly composed as she almost always was, in her favorite red dress and overcoat. She offered a charming smile to every person they passed on their way.

Marcella strode with confidence. Gloved hands shoved in the pockets of the pants she wore. She wore a brimmed hat that was pulled down to hide her face from anyone looking down at her. Her knees might have been shaking, but none would know she was afraid.

Alma wore a flower pattern dress that complimented the black shawl over her shoulders. Held in both hands in front of her she carried a knitting bag. It held extra needles and wool traps.

They were armored and armed for what they all knew would be the hardest fight of their lives.

They entered the building with no fanfare. The main lobby was full of men and women. Many seemed to be leaving for the day, but others still rushed about with the urgency of workers on a task.

Melissa closed her umbrella and took the lead. She stopped at the information desk and smiled warmly at the young woman standing behind it.

"Can I help you?" she asked.

"Yes," Melissa answered. "We're here to see Mr. Chelsea."

The woman's expression became confused for a moment before she forced the smile back. "Do you have an appointment?"

Before any of them could answer the phone on the desk rang.

"I'm sorry, just a moment." The receptionist picked up the phone.

She listened for a moment. "Of course. I'll let them know."

She hung up the phone and smiled at them again. "Looks like he was expecting you. You can take any of the elevators to the top floor. He's ready for your meeting."

All three of them felt their blood turn to ice. "Thank you," Melissa said and they made their way to the elevators.

"That can't be good," Marcy whispered.

"At least we don't have to go looking for him," Melissa replied.

They waited patiently for a set of doors to slide open and walked onto the elevator.

Alma took a deep breath before pushing the button for the top floor. "Cast on."

THE MOOD in the math room was somber. Johan was pacing, Beans alert on his bed watching him walk back and forth. Felicia was scribbling furiously on her paper, new cap pulled tight on her head.

Abigail sat in a chair running her hand through the large bag of wool at her feet. There had been a lot of failed attempts mixing elements that Alma could use in her knitting. The wool was still toowerver, but not perfect.

Felicia cursed and hurled her chewed on pencil across the room at the screen of scrolling numbers.

"What is it?" Johan asked, stopping his pacing.

Felicia held her face in her hands, shoulders shaking from sudden, uncontrollable sobbing. "They're going to die!"

"You don't know that," Johan argued.

"Yes I do!" She dropped to the ground and jabbed accusingly at the numbers on the screen. "I know exactly what's going to happen! He knows they're coming. He saw us. The math, it says he's ready for them."

"Just for them?" Abigail asked.

"Who else? They're the hunters. He doesn't have to worry about us. But..." She shook her head. "It doesn't matter. He's going to kill them and there's nothing we can do about it. Then he's going to kill the whole city."

"What do you mean?" Abigail said, slowly rising from her seat.

"The math says that he's going to feed on the city and move on. There are so many more Ravel that we didn't find. We missed them. All of them. He's going to set them free and just, move on. Like he always does."

"No." Abigail bent down and picked up her bag of wool. "Not today. Not ever. He's not getting away again."

"What do you think you can do?" Felicia asked, face twisted in a cruel smile. "We lost."

"You don't have all the numbers, Fey." Abigail crossed the distance between them and pulled Felicia into a hug.

The other girl let out a surprised gasp before wrapping her own arms around Abigail.

Abigail let her cry for a moment before holding her out at arms length and meeting her eye. "Can you trust me?"

Felicia nodded.

"Are you and Beans going to be okay if Johan and I leave you alone?"

Another nod.

"Great. Johan, I need you to get me to them. We're going to save them."

"How?" Johan asked. "I'm not a fighter."

"No, but you can drive. That's all I need you to do." She held up her bag. "I've got this."

THE ELEVATOR DOORS opened and Alma, Melissa, and Marcella stepped out into a large room that gleamed of metal and glass. The windows were large and offered an unrivaled view of the city.

The polished metal of the floor was occasionally

broken by uncomfortable looking armchairs or a long table.

The far end of the room was dominated by a massive black desk behind which sat Ald Chelsea.

He was reclining in his office chair, feet up on the desk and a newspaper open in front of him.

He flipped the paper down at the sound of the door opening and smiled at the three women.

"Ah, you must be, let's see," he snapped his fingers as he tried to remember, "Ah, yes. Alma, Melissa, and Marcella, right?"

They all stopped and stared in surprise.

"Yes. I have a very good team working for me. Found out everything I could ever want to know. Apparently I killed your families." He stood up and shrugged. "Oops."

"We're here to kill you," Alma announced.

"I'm sure you're here to try. Been a long time since anyone's discovered who I am. *What* I am. I'm impressed. I suspect it's the scrawny redhead that figured it out. According to my sources she's the real brains behind everything."

He rounded the desk, slowly removing his suit coat and rolling up the sleeves of his shirt. "Well, did we want to just get this over with? Or did you want to give me a whole speech about how I ruined your lives and all that nonsense."

Marcy let out an angry roar and charged. She moved much quicker than she ever had before. The new gloves worked perfectly. She was almost as fast now as Melissa had been with her old scarf.

She jumped and swung a kick at Ald's face.

One instant he was staring ahead, hands in his pockets, the next one arm was up blocking the kick and the other was stretched out, hand around Marcy's throat.

"Points for the effort." With a casual flick of his wrist he threw her across the room where she bounced off a window, leaving a web of cracks in the thick glass.

"So much anger," Ald said, smile spreading. "I love it. I should warn you, in the name of fair play, I am about to be getting a whole lot stronger."

Melissa and Alma froze in their own charges at that announcement.

"You see, I knew that you knew about me. I don't like that. I don't know if you've told anyone. So, it's time to move on. You did a decent job clearing out that nest in the sewers, but that was just one of several I have hidden around the city. Biggest one is actually under this building. So doing a little cleanup here at corporate. Can you imagine all the pain and fear that's just going to be rolling up here once hundreds of people start dying? Not to mention what happens once they've finished here and moved out into the city? Whoo boy, I'm going to be very full." He grinned, too white teeth stark against the black of his shirt.

"You monster." Alma pulled her hand from her bag with two long needles. She dropped the bag and charged.

Ald casually dodged every swing of her weapons.

Across the room Melissa was checking on Marcy who groaned but seemed to have escaped serous injury. The shawl had worked.

Ald sidestepped another stab and grabbed Alma's wrist. "I feel I should let you know, I sent one of my birds to take care of the three you left behind. I suspect it's getting there about now."

Alma's eyes opened wide in shock and anger.

Ald didn't manage to dodge the next needle that stabbed through his vest right where his heart would be.

It bent.

"I liked this shirt." His voice lost its conversational tone. He backhanded Alma on the cheek and sent the woman spinning through the air.

Melissa dove and caught Alma before she crashed into the long conference table along one of the walls.

Alma rose, wiping blood away from her lip. The shawl had managed to stop most of the hit, but the sheer strength of it had overridden most of the defenses. And that had just been a casual slap.

"Don't let him hit you," she warned.

"Yeah," Melissa agreed.

"We attack together. Okay?"

Marcy grunted her agreement.

"Then let's go."

They charged together.

FELICIA AND BEANS sat in the dark of the math room. She'd turned the screen off. She wouldn't be needing the numbers anymore. She already knew how the night was going to end.

She touched the wool of the hat on her head and took a deep breath. It was about time.

"It's going to be okay, Beansie," she said to the dog.

He whined, sensing her apprehension.

"At least Abigail and Johan got out. I think they're going to be okay."

Both dog and girl turned at a sound outside the door.

The door knob turned. It took several attempts before the unpracticed hand managed to turn it all the way and push the door open.

The white face of a Magpie entered first. It tilted side to side, inspecting the room before focusing on Felicia. Then the rest of its frame followed. It had to turn itself to get in through the door. The room was too small for it to open its wings, but it still made for an intimidating display as it straightened itself, the bone mask almost touching the ceiling.

Felicia sighed. Behind her the room's second door was open and she whistled to Beans who was standing at attention, hackles raised.

The dog looked to her and whined a complaint, but she whistled again and he ran through the open door.

The Magpie watched him go before turning back to Felicia.

Felicia took a swig from a half finished energy drink on the table before dropping the can on the floor. It rolled a few feet toward the Magpie.

"Well?" Felicia asked it. "Are you going to do it or not?"

It took a step forward and stopped. Glancing down it

cocked its head to the side and studied the small ball of knitted wool that it had stepped on. It had been under a wrapper from Felicia's favorite restaurant

The wool traps were one of Alma's specialties. This particular one was what happened when the woman tried to knit together toowerver wool of Fire and Water.

The ball of soft fabric exploded in a geyser of steam that caused the Magpie to scream in shock and pain.

Felicia dropped from the table and darted out the doorway after Beans.

The Magpie stumbled forward out of the curtain of steam intent on completing the mission given by its master. Its taloned foot fell on the can Felicia had rolled toward it.

Another surprised cry came out as it slipped forward.

Its head hit the table at just the right angle, just like Felicia's math had predicted.

The bone mask protected its head from any real harm, but there was still a snap as its neck broke from the fall.

"Huh," Felicia said as she and Beans peered around the doorway into the room. "I wasn't completely sure that would work."

JOHAN'S DRIVING was nothing short of incredible. Speed and precision. He wove in and out of traffic as though he were knitting his own pattern.

They arrived at the Chelsea Industries building in record time.

"Should the power be off?" Abigail asked as they both jumped out of the truck and rushed toward the front door.

They could hear sirens in the distance.

"I get the feeling it was planned, yeah." Johan sprinted in front of her and pushed the doors.

They didn't budge.

"Oh, Shepherd's Crook," he cursed, stepping back away from the door.

Abigail moved closer and peered inside. "Oh."

Ravel. So many Ravel. Houndling and Dracons moved around the lobby, sifting through the remains of what had once been people. Up higher flew an entire flock of Magpies.

"We can't do this," Johan said. He cursed again and slammed his fist against the door. "They're in there, Abi. We have to help them. But... but we can't."

Abigail laid a gentle hand on his shoulder. "Step back."

He did as she asked.

She reached into her bag and pulled out a skein of wool. This a combination of Earth and Fire.

She pulled out an arm's length strand. She placed the end on one side of the door and willed the Earth to hold it in place. She stretched the rest of the length across the door and did the same on the other side. She slid a pair of scissors from her bag and cut it away from the skein.

"Cover your ears," she told Johan.

He gave her a confused look but did as she asked.

She released the string and covered her own ears. Then allowed the elements inside that short length of string to do their thing.

The wool dissolved, and then the door exploded inward.

Several Houndlings and Dracons were caught in the blast and shredded by the glass and steel shrapnel of the door.

"Stay behind me," Abigail said as she strode into the room. She held the skein of Earth and Fire in one hand, bag dangling from the crook of her arm, and the scissors in the other.

She held the wool in front of her face and pulled up an inch long piece then quickly snipped it off. With a quick breath she launched it away from her.

She channeled the Earth in the severed piece, granting it a more substantial weight, and it flew like a thrown pebble straight toward the mass of Ravel charging toward her and Johan.

The explosion wasn't as large as the one she'd used to open the door, but it rocked the room and instantly killed the Houndlings that had charged past the wool.

She stepped forward into the open space the explosion had cleared and began to pull and cut inch long pieces in rapid succession. She blew them in every direction.

Houndlings and Dracon were incinerated and shred apart with every explosion.

"Abigail!" Johan shouted, his voice hard to hear over the ringing in her ears. "The Magpies!"

She quickly looked up and saw the diving figures.

She pulled another arm's length piece and snipped it free. Spinning it above her head she released it with another long breath and the circle of wool floated up slowly, somehow resisting the down draft of the Magpie wings.

Magpies were smarter than other Ravel and several let out cries of alarm and tried to retreat.

Abigail and Johan both dropped to the ground as the ring of wool exploded outward. Only the space directly beneath it wasn't filled with incinerating fire.

The two of them rose and continued their slow march through the lobby.

The Houndlings and Dracons recognized the danger now and attempted to flee but Abigail was merciless. By the time she and Johan made it to the stairs there was nothing else alive in the lobby. There was also no more of her Fire and Earth Skein.

"Why didn't you tell us you could do this?" Johan asked.

She shrugged. "You didn't ask."

Halfway up the stairs they encountered another Magpie.

Abigail pulled another roll of yarn from her bag, this one Air and Water. Instead of using the scissors she simply flipped out a length of it and whipped it toward the Magpie. It wrapped around the monster's throat as though it were an actual whip and not a length of wool.

She yanked down and the Magpie hit the handrail before falling down the stairwell clawing at the binding around its neck. Abigail didn't move fast enough and the Skein was pulled from her hand.

They met no other resistance as they ran up the stairs.

Johan faired better than Abigail and she assumed it was because of the toowerver socks he wore. But they both managed to make it to the top of the building thanks to adrenaline and their desire to save their friends.

Johan reached the door first and shouldered it open.

Inside the office their friends fought.

Alma was running around Ald and tossing the small knit balls that she called her traps.

The balls were bouncing off Ald and exploding in bursts of steam or showers of mud that didn't seem to be slowing him down at all.

He marched through the distractions toward Marcy, who lay on the ground cradling her left arm that seemed to be bent in an unnatural angle.

"Leave her alone!" Melissa shouted, rising from the remains of a shattered conference table.

The scarf around her neck floated up in its normal fashion, but a soft glow began to emanate from within its fibers and she moved so fast that no one in the room could really see what happened.

She dashed past Ald, swinging her umbrella like a sword. The blade tip slashed through the fabric of his vest and shirt but did nothing to the stone of his flesh.

She was moving too fast to stop properly so she

simply jumped, feet first toward the wall. She connected with a crunch of breaking glass and launched herself back toward the Selvage. Again she slashed at him as she flew past.

Again and again she did this, dashing and rebounding off the walls or ceiling or floor, every time slashing the man.

But Ald kept moving, seeming to ignore the attacks of blade and trap alike.

He held up a hand and there was a pained scream as he caught Melissa by her face.

Blood poured from her freshly broken nose as Ald held her aloft, her entire head fitting inside the palm of his hand.

Her umbrella fell from limp fingers and the unfelt wind of her scarf vanished as it fell limp and lifeless around her neck.

He tossed her aside and she slid to a stop amid the ruins of the conference table she'd so recently emerged from. She lay, unmoving.

Ald laughed as he kicked her umbrella out of his way and continued his slow march toward Marcella.

"You—" Alma began a curse as she charged him with two needles raised to stab but was cut off as Ald spun on her and drove a fist into her stomach.

"What's that?" he demanded. "What am I?"

"Their shawls?" Johan said as Abigail pushed her way past him. "Why aren't they—"

"Even toowerver wool has its limits," Abigail answered gently as she strode into the room.

"Hey!" she shouted just as Ald was raising a second fist to drive into the top of Alma's head.

The woman had fallen to her knees, blood running from her mouth.

"Ah, the farmer's daughter, correct?" Ald asked, turning away from the now prone Alma. "Didn't really get much information on you." He paused and tilted his head to the side. "I'm getting a lot of anger from you, but not the same as theirs. I haven't killed anyone you love have I? Forgive me if I forgot, I kill a lot of loved ones."

"No. You've just hurt my friends."

"Ah. But of course. Don't worry. I'll end the suffering. To be quite honest, I'm actually rather full at the moment."

"You're right. It's all going to end very quickly." Abigail reached into her bag and pulled out her final roll of yarn. It was the first she'd done for Alma. Her test. Every few lengths a different color. A different element or combination.

The first length was orange, the Fire she'd started with. She flung it out like a whip. Just as she had against the last Magpie.

"What are you, Agh!" Ald started with a laugh that ended with a pained scream as the whip snapped across his face.

He touched his cheek with a hand and pulled it away bloody. A short, smoking gash broke his face.

"A draaier." He shook his head. "Been a while since I've seen one of you. But I'll have—"

Abigail didn't let him talk. She kept spinning her

whip and moving in closer. With every snap and spark of fire a small length of the wool vanished, but Ald was pushed back a step or two.

"Enough!" He bellowed and jumped in toward her.

She stepped back, spinning the wool in front of her making an impassible disk of flame.

Then the last of the Fire burned out.

She cursed and dove to the side as he smashed the ground where she'd been standing with a powerful fist.

She began to rapidly unspool the wool and threw a handful toward him.

She willed the Earth to weigh a small section of fibers down and the Air to move others.

Loops of wool shot up around Ald Chelsea. They wrapped around his wrists and he bellowed with rage and confusion as he tried to tear himself free but found he couldn't.

Soon Abigail was holding one end of the wool as the rest was wrapped around Ald like a cocoon.

"Someone please do something!" she shouted, hoping that Melissa or Marcy had managed to find their feet.

Behind her Melissa rose, staggering to her feet. She bent down and picked up her umbrella and made her way in a weaving line toward Ald.

"This is for my family," she managed through the curtain of blood still pouring from her nose.

She stabbed once into Ald's heart. Still unable to break his skin, but he winced at the blow. And again, in the exact same spot. She never realized she was screaming, and no one would ever tell her. It just wasn't like her to lose her composure like that.

Knit. A stab to the chest. Knit. Another. Knit. Again. Knit, knit, knit. Knit. Knit. Knit. Knit.

Ald screamed as the skin broke and the umbrella found purchase. Melissa fell to the side, balance she'd barely managed to find lost. From behind her Marcella charged, left arm dangling uselessly at her side, her own feral cry parting her lips.

She punched with everything she had in her. With everything her gloves had to offer. With all her anger and sorrow and fear. She drove the point of the umbrella through Ald's heart.

BIND OFF

THEY MANAGED to leave the building before the authorities arrived. The Ravel popping up all around the city had apparently kept them occupied. But with the death of Ald all fight had gone out of the monsters.

Alma had said it was because the Selvage had made the Ravel and the creatures couldn't function without one to lead them. The Magpies, maybe, but those had apparently fled immediately after Ald's death.

Someone from the city had come by and collected the Magpie corpse in the math room so they didn't have too much clean up to do.

None of them had the energy to do anything other than sit and stare at each other.

They'd stopped by the hospital, but with the Ravel attacks the doctors hadn't had time for too many patients. Marcy's arm had been put in a cast and they'd checked Alma for internal injuries, then kicked them out the door to make room for more seriously injured people.

"What are you going to do now?" Abigail asked from her position on her back on the cool cement of the warehouse floor.

"There are other Selvages out there," Alma answered without elaboration.

"But Ald was the one you were after," Marcella said. "The one that killed our families. Do we really care about the others?" Her left arm was in a sling.

Alma shrugged. "I don't know what else I'd do."

"You could stay here for a while?" Abigail offered.

Melissa smiled at that. She'd set her own nose and now half her face was wrapped in bandages. "I wouldn't mind slowing down for a little while."

"Yeah, that doesn't really sound awful," Johan added. "I'd definitely be up for sticking around for a bit." He met Abigail's eyes and they both smiled sheepishly.

"Ah, gack." Marcy made a gagging noise.

"I think staying would be good, too." Felicia sat perched on a box, Beans head resting on her lap.

Alma sighed. "Okay. We'll stay."

They all gave what might have been a cheer if they hadn't been emotionally and physically drained.

"I could use some time to work on my knitting anyway."

The End

ABOUT THE AUTHOR

James is a South African born writer with an American accent, because children are cruel and laughed at the way he said "orange."

He was the last kid in his class to learn to read, so once that was remedied he quickly made up for lost time and read everything he could get his hands on.

Eventually someone said, "Hey, James, read this fantasy novel." He did, and still hasn't managed to crawl out of that rabbit hole, though he has found others to fall into.

The first story he ever wrote was horrible but everyone pretended it was great, so now he can't feel good about himself unless someone is praising his work.

He lives in Utah with a dog and a growing collection of porch cats.